GEORGE FOREMAN
Let George Do It!

GEORGE FOREMAN
Let George Do It!

BY

GEORGE FOREMAN
AND *FRAN MANUSHKIN*

ILLUSTRATED BY

WHITNEY MARTIN

Simon & Schuster Books for Young Readers
New York   London   Toronto   Sydney

SIMON & SCHUSTER BOOKS FOR YOUNG READERS

An imprint of Simon & Schuster Children's Publishing Division

1230 Avenue of the Americas, New York, New York 10020

Text copyright © 2005 by George Foreman

Illustrations copyright © 2005 by Whitney Martin

SIMON & SCHUSTER BOOKS FOR YOUNG READERS is a trademark of

Simon & Schuster, Inc.

Book design by Dan Potash

The text for this book is set in Hadriano.

The illustrations for this book are rendered in watercolor.

Manufactured in the United States of America

2 4 6 8 10 9 7 5 3 1

Library of Congress Cataloging-in-Publication Data

Foreman, George, 1949–

Let George do it! / George Foreman and Fran Manushkin ; illustrated by Whitney Martin.—1st ed.

p. cm.

Summary: Five brothers named George, along with Mrs. George,

get ready for Big George's birthday party.

ISBN 0-689-87807-9 (hardcover)

[1. Names, Personal—Fiction. 2. Parties—Fiction. 3. Birthdays—Fiction.]

I. Manushkin, Fran. II. Martin, Whitney, 1968– ill. III. Title.

PZ7.F75817Le 2005

[E]—dc22

2004010156

first
edition

I would like to dedicate this book to the memory of my father,
J. D. Foreman, who gave me something to be proud of,
which no one can ever take away: the name "Foreman."
A name is what you make of it.—G. F.

For my great nephew, Jonah Otto Engelmann—F. M.

To my boys, Roddy and Whitney, with love, and in loving
memory of my father, Marvin Roderick Martin—W. M.

Thanks to Mary Martelly Foreman, my wife, who
has done all she could to keep our ten kids a family.

Thanks to God for our five boys, who have never
asked, "Why do we have the same name—George?"

And last, thanks to Miriam Altshuler, who has always
helped me get to where I wanted to go in writing.—G. F.

Thank you to Big George for a fun story
and for letting me take a swing at the pictures.

And to Terese for helping me get to the twelfth round.—W. M.

"Good morning, George."

"Good morning, George."

"Good morning, George."

"Good morning, George."

"Today is Big George's birthday. Can I count on all of you to help with the party?" Mrs. George asked her sons.

"You bet," said George, George, George, and George.

"Urgle," said Baby George.

George made the cake.

George vacuumed.

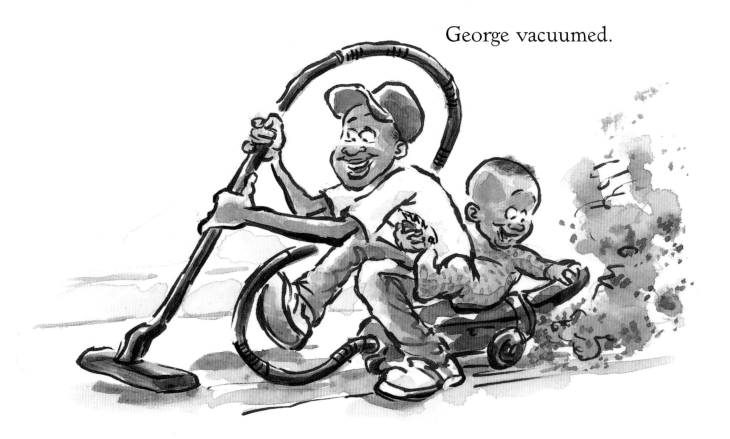

George put up decorations.

George took out the trash,

and George took a nap.

"Package for George!" called the deliveryman.

"I bet it's your birthday present!" said George.

George, George, George, George, and Big George came running.

"It's for George."

George vacuumed.

George carried down
the extra chairs.

George bathed the baby,

and George gathered flowers
from the garden.

"Phone call for George!" called Mrs. George.

She tossed the phone to Big George,

who tossed it to George,

who tossed it to George.

who tossed it to George,

who tossed it to George,

"Wrong number!"

Everyone got busy again.

What are these chairs doing here? wondered George, and he brought them back up.

George put up decorations.

George bathed the baby,

and George vacuumed.

"Package for George!" called the deliveryman.

Big George, George, George,
George, and George came running.

"It's for George," said George.

"Wait!" yelled George. "Isn't there another box for George?"
"Let me see," said the deliveryman. "Yes, here it is."

"You rescued my present!" Big George said.
"Let's call him . . . George."

"Do you like it?" asked George, George, George, and George.
"Of course," said Big George. "You can never have too many Georges."

Everyone hurried inside to get dressed for the party. "This place is a mess," said George.

He vacuumed the floor,

and brought down the party chairs,

and bathed the baby.

At the party, George told his dad,
"Remember, any time you need help—"

"Let George do it!"